The Dreaming Tree

For Erica.
A.B.

For Alice.
Also with thanks to Colette and Tom.
C.F.

First published in Great Britain by HarperCollins*Publishers* Ltd 2000
1 3 5 7 9 10 8 6 4 2

Text © Alan Brown 2000
Illustrations © Claire Fletcher 2000

ISBN 0 00 198321 0

The HarperCollins website address is: www.fireandwater.com.

Printed in Hong Kong.

The Dreaming Tree

Alan Brown

illustrated by Claire Fletcher

Collins

An imprint of HarperCollinsPublishers

My name is Erica, and I live in the town, in a long row of little houses that all look the same. There are only paving stones at the front, and a tiny yard at the back. My friends tease me for being a dreamer, because I am always thinking about wild places far away. But I know that dreams sometimes do come true.

My favourite place for dreaming used to be under
the wild cherry tree at the end of our street.

One day in spring, I was sitting under the blossom-laden
branches, dreaming that I was walking amongst snowy
mountains. In my mind, the beep of car horns in the street
around me became the sound of goat bells rising from the
valley. As I looked up, the petals of the cherry tree turned
into soft white snowflakes, falling on my face.

My dream was broken by a man in a suit who was pinning a notice on the cherry tree.

"We're going to widen this road," he said.

"Oh, but what will happen to the tree?" I cried.

"We'll chop it down," said the man cheerfully, "before the year is out."

The end of the cherry tree and all my dreaming! I put my arms around the tree and felt its rough bark against the palms of my hands. Tears filled my eyes like melting snow. Right then I made up my mind. I was going to save the cherry tree.

I went to my brother Steve for help.

"Let's get people to ask for the tree to stay," I said to him. "They won't dare cut it down if we all want it."

"OK," said Steve. "We'll give it a try."

Summer came. As I sat under the cherry tree, quarrelsome birds scrabbled for fruit in its branches. I dreamed I was pushing through a steamy jungle, and the falling cherry stones became rain drops dripping through the leaves. The birds turned into gaudy parrots, squawking and whistling in lofty tree tops.

At the end of our street, I asked shoppers to sign my paper that said, "Save our cherry tree!" Steve was shy about asking at first, but soon we were doing it together. The people were very kind, and we got lots of names.

Autumn came. As the golden sun shone on the flaming red and yellow cherry leaves, I dreamed I was wandering across the tawny plains of Africa. The footsteps of people became the thunder of zebras' hooves, and the sound of traffic turned into the roar of hunting lions, racing through the long grasses.

Dad helped me carry the list of names to Mrs Malik at the Town Hall. There were pages and pages of paper, and it was very big and heavy.

"Please don't let them chop down our cherry tree," I said to her. "Lots of people want to save it, but only someone important like you can do it."

"I'll see what I can do," said Mrs Malik, gently.

It was winter, and no word came from Mrs Malik.

As I sat under the cherry tree, the wind thrashed the branches and wet leaves fell on my face. I dreamed I was walking in bare feet on coral sands, far away on a tropical island. The wind and the rain became waves crashing and splashing on the shore, and the falling leaves turned into dolphins leaping high out of a sparkling blue sea.

Very early one frosty morning, I heard the noise of huge machines. I looked out of my window. The cherry tree was so beautiful in the rising sun. Suddenly, I saw that workmen were putting tapes across the road to stop the traffic. They were going to chop down my dreaming tree! Had no one seen the petition after all?

I dashed out of the house, and Steve followed me. We raced down the street, yelling to each other,

"It's a protest! It's a demo!"

Every child in the street came running out to join us. We were in our nightclothes but we didn't feel the cold, we were so excited.

We all joined hands in a big circle round the cherry tree. I was crying with happiness, because my friends were helping me. I was crying with fear for the tree.

"Hands off our tree!" we all shouted together.

The workmen could not get past. "All right, kids," they laughed, "we'll just have a cup of tea," and they stood by their machines with mugs in their hands.

"You are very good at organising things, Erica," said an important-looking lady.

"Mrs Malik!" I ran to her. "You're just in time to stop them chopping down the cherry tree!"

"I'm very sorry, Erica, but it is in the way and has to go," said Mrs Malik, firmly.

I had no tears left to cry. Then I realised that the workmen were not chopping down the cherry tree. They were digging it up, roots and all. The machine I thought was going to destroy the tree was gently scooping it up in enormous jaws.

"Come on!" said Mrs Malik. We all hurried after her and the tree was carried at the front of a procession of children, down the road towards the little house where I live. The workmen dug a big hole in the middle of the paving stones. Then the man in the machine planted the cherry tree right in front of my house! I was so happy, I hugged everybody, and I saved the biggest hug of all for Dad. He gave me a kiss. "You're the one who did it, Erica. Now you can dream under your cherry tree every day, and your dreams will last all night long."

It is the end of a long year, the year we saved the cherry tree. The branches are covered in snow and hung with bright coloured lights. And that's how I know that dreams really can come true.